Disney
Winnie the Pooh
Tales of
Kindness

DISNEP PRESS

LOS ANGELES • NEW YORK

Contents

Written by **Nancy Parent**
Illustrated by the **Disney Storybook Art Team**

Pooh's Kindness Game

Eeyore is hungry.

He eats flowers!

But there is a rock in his way.

Eeyore tries to push the rock.
There is a stack of rocks
behind him.
Eeyore does not see the stack.
It starts to fall!

A big rock falls on Eeyore's tail.
"Oh, well," says Eeyore.

Piglet walks by.

"Oh, dear!" he says.

"Let me help you."

Piglet tries to push the rock.
It is too big.
"I think I am stuck,"
says Eeyore.

Piglet goes for help.
He knocks on
Winnie the Pooh's door.

"Hurry!" says Piglet.
"Eeyore needs our help."

Pooh and Piglet run to
help Eeyore.
Rabbit and Tigger
come along, too.

"What happened?"
asks Rabbit.
"Just lucky, I guess,"
says Eeyore.

Everyone works together.

They push.

They pull.

Eeyore is free!
Everyone cheers.
"Thanks," says Eeyore.
"That feels better."

Just then, Owl flies over.

"Hello there!" he calls.

"I could use some help."

Everyone follows Owl to his house.

"What is wrong?" Tigger asks.
"I cannot find my glasses,"
says Owl.

The friends look up and down.
They look over and under.
They do not find the glasses.

"Excuse me," Pooh says to Owl.
"But are your glasses
on your head?"

Owl feels silly.

"Oh!" he says.

"How kind of you, Pooh."

"Hooray!" says Tigger.
"We helped two friends."

"Helping makes me hungry,"
says Pooh.
Pooh and Piglet start
to walk home.

They walk by Kanga
and Roo's house.

"Can you help me?" Roo asks.
"I think my swing is broken."

"I may be a bear
of very little brain,"
says Pooh.
"But I think you just
need a push."

"I can almost touch the sky!"
says Roo.
"Thank you, Pooh!"

Pooh and Piglet wave goodbye.
Then they go home for a snack.

More friends come over for tea.
They talk about their day.
Everyone liked
helping each other.

Pooh has an idea.
He calls it the Kindness Game.
"We can do one kind thing
every day," he says.

The next day, Pooh starts
to play the Kindness Game.
"Piglet will like this basket,"
says Pooh.

Pooh gives Piglet the basket.
"Thank you, Pooh!" says Piglet.
"It is the perfect gift."

The next day, it is Rabbit's turn
to play the Kindness Game.
He brings Pooh honey.

The next day, it is Tigger's turn
to play the Kindness Game.
He helps Rabbit in the garden.

"Who knew hard work
was so much fun?"
says Tigger.

The next day, it is Piglet's turn
to play the Kindness Game.
He makes muffins for
Kanga and Roo.

The next day, it is Eeyore's turn
to play the Kindness Game.
He and Tigger play
Pooh Sticks.

The next day, the friends
meet at Pooh's house.

Everyone feels very happy.
Even Eeyore is smiling!

"It must be
the Kindness Game!"
says Pooh.

Kindness is good for everyone,
and good for you, too!

Hooray for Winnie the Pooh
and the Kindness Game!

Who Cares?
Pooh Cares!

It is a sunny day.
A mother duck
watches her eggs.

CRACK! CRACK! CRACK!
The eggs break open.

The mother now has
three babies!
"Quack, quack!" they say.
They go for a swim.

CRACK!

One more egg breaks open.
The last baby is all alone.

Winnie the Pooh is
out on a walk.
He asks Piglet to come along.

They walk by the pond.
"Quack, quack!"
"What is that?" Piglet asks.

Pooh and Piglet find
the baby duck.
"Where is her mother?"
Pooh asks.

Pooh and Piglet look around.
They do not see
the mother duck.

"We cannot leave her alone,"
says Piglet.
"Follow us, little one!"
says Pooh.

"That is the perfect name,"
says Piglet.

"We can call her Little."

"What do ducks like to eat?"
Pooh asks.
"I do not know," says Piglet.
"But Rabbit has a lot of
good things to eat."

The next day, they go to
Rabbit's house.
Rabbit has a big garden.
He grows vegetables.

Little likes the vegetables.
"Thank you, Rabbit,"
says Piglet.

"Now we must be going.
We need to find
Little's mother," says Pooh.

CONDENSED
MILK

They walk by Kanga and Roo.
"This is Little," says Pooh.
"We are looking for
her mother."

"Little is even littler than I am!" says Roo.

"Come play with me, Little!"

Roo is happy to have
a new friend.
He teaches her
his favorite games.

Roo and Little find
a mud puddle.
They make mud pies.

Then they need a bath!
Little likes the bubbles.

Little's feathers are
wet and fuzzy.
Owl shows her how
to dry them.

They walk by Tigger.
"Who is the new bird?"
he asks.

"This is Little," says Roo.
"We are looking for
her mother."

They go to the pond.
Little makes new friends.

"Little is a lot of fun!"
says Tigger.

Tigger shows Little
how to bounce.
"First, you get down real low,"
he explains.

"Then you bounce up high!"
says Tigger.

"Quack, quack!"
says Little.

Eeyore walks by.

Little waddles over to him.

"Can you show me
how to do that?"
Eeyore asks.

They go for a waddle.
Eeyore trips and falls!
Little helps him up.

"I think we are lost,"
says Eeyore.
"Someone will come by soon."

Eeyore and Little fall asleep.
Pooh and Piglet find them.

"Quack, quack!"
"What is that?"
asks Eeyore.

"Look!" says Piglet.
"A duck family."
"Could that be Little's mother?"
asks Pooh.

Little swims over to her family.
"Quack, quack!" they say.

"It IS Little's mother!"
says Piglet.

Pooh gives his new little friend
a big hug goodbye.

The Forgiving Friend

Rabbit works in his garden every day.
He grows a lot of food.
Today he needs help.

Everyone comes to help.
"Many hands make light work!"
says Rabbit.

"Look at all this food!"
says Tigger.

Everyone works hard.
"Thank you," says Rabbit.
"You can take some
food home."

"But we are not done,"
says Piglet.
"We will come back
again tomorrow."

Winnie the Pooh and Piglet
walk by Kanga and
Roo's house.

They stop to say hello.
Roo does not feel well.

"Mama's garden soup
makes me feel better,"
says Roo.

But Kanga does not have
any garden soup.

"There is more food in
Rabbit's garden," says Piglet.

But Rabbit is not home.
"I do not think he will mind,"
says Piglet.

Piglet brings the food
to Kanga.
"Thank you, Piglet!"
says Kanga.

Rabbit comes home with
Tigger, Eeyore, and Owl.

The garden is empty.
Where is the food?

"Did you take all the food
from the garden?"
Tigger asks Rabbit.

"Do not be silly!"
says Rabbit.

"Did you take all the food
from the garden?"
Tigger asks Owl.

"No, I did not,"
says Owl.

"Did you take all the
food from the garden?"
Tigger asks Eeyore.
"No, I did not,"
says Eeyore.

"Did you take all the food
from the garden?"
Tigger asks Pooh.
"No, I did not,"
says Pooh.

Tigger thinks.

"Did you take all the food
from the garden?"
Pooh asks Tigger.

"Did I take all the food from the garden?" Tigger asks himself.

Tigger looks all over
his house.
He does not find
the food.

"Did you take all the food
from the garden?"
Tigger asks Kanga.

"No," says Kanga.

"Piglet gave it to me."

"I knew it was Piglet!"
says Tigger.

"I found the food
from the garden!"
says Tigger.
"Piglet gave it to Kanga."

Rabbit is surprised.
"Piglet should have asked me,"
he says.

Piglet brings Rabbit muffins.
"I am sorry," he says.
"I did not think you would mind.
Next time I will ask
before taking."

"It is okay,"
says Rabbit.
"I forgive you."

Everyone brings food to share.
"Forgiveness is tasty!"
says Tigger.

Rabbit does not stay angry.
He is a forgiving friend.

What Good Friends Do

Piglet hears noises
all around him.
He cannot sleep.
He is scared of monsters.

The next day, Winnie the Pooh
goes to Piglet's house.

Pooh opens the door.
Piglet is still in bed.

"I could not sleep," says Piglet.
"I heard monsters all night."

Pooh and Piglet look
under the table.
There are no monsters.
They look under the bed.
There are no monsters.

Piglet is still scared.

"Maybe a snack will
help us feel brave,"
says Pooh.

Piglet makes tea.
There is a loud *HISS*.

"No need to be scared,"
says Pooh.
The noise is just the teapot.

There is a loud
DRIP, DRIP, DROP.
Piglet hides under a chair.

"No need to be scared,"
says Pooh.
The noise is just the sink.

Pooh wants to help
his friend.
"What if you try
to be brave?"
he asks Piglet.

Piglet does not know how.

Pooh will help him.

That is what good friends do.

It starts to rain.

The rain makes a lot of noise.

"Can I try to be
brave tomorrow?"
Piglet asks.

Pooh will sleep over tonight.
He will help Piglet be brave.
That is what good friends do.

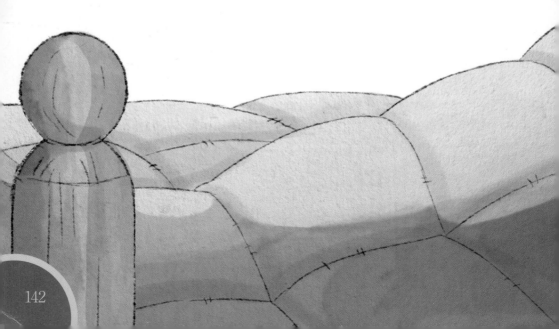

Soon Piglet hears a loud
SNORE.

He follows the noise.

The noise is just Pooh.
Piglet goes back to bed.

The next day, Pooh and Piglet
go for a walk.

They hear a loud
"HOO-HOO-HOO!"
"No need to be scared,"
says Pooh.

The noise is just Tigger.
Piglet feels silly.

Piglet sees a butterfly.
He stops to look at it.

Piglet turns around.

Pooh is gone!

Piglet is scared.

Piglet hears a noise.

He covers his eyes.

"Be brave, be brave, be brave,"
Piglet says to himself.

It is just Kanga.
She is looking for Roo.

Piglet hears more noises.
But he is not scared.

He keeps walking.
"There you are, Pooh!"
says Piglet.

"I tried to be brave,"
says Piglet.

"That was a very
brave thing to do,"
says Pooh.

Pooh helped Piglet be brave.
That is what good friends do.

5